This story was inspired by the wildlife film *Reflections on Elephants* from the series
The Savage Paradise, a National Geographic Production produced by Wildlife Films, Botswana.

The author would like to thank Dr Gerald Legg of the
Booth Museum of Natural History, Brighton, for his help and advice.

VIKING/PUFFIN

Published by the Penguin Group
Penguin Books Ltd, 27 Wrights Lane, London W8 5TZ, England
Penguin Putnam Inc., 375 Hudson Street, New York, New York 10014, USA
Penguin Books Australia Ltd, Ringwood, Victoria, Australia
Penguin Books Canada Ltd, 10 Alcorn Avenue, Toronto, Ontario, Canada M4V 3B2
Penguin Books (NZ) Ltd, Private Bag 102902, NSMC, Auckland, New Zealand

Penguin Books Ltd, Registered Offices: Harmondsworth, Middlesex, England

First published in Viking 1997
5 7 9 10 8 6

Published in Puffin Books 1998
5 7 9 10 8 6 4

Text copyright © Theresa Radcliffe, 1997
Illustrations copyright © John Butler, 1997

The moral right of the author and illustrator has been asserted

Made and printed in Italy by Printer Trento srl

British Library Cataloguing in Publication Data
A CIP catalogue record for this book is available from the British Library

ISBN 0–670–87054–4 Hardback
ISBN 0–140–55913–2 Paperback

THERESA RADCLIFFE

BASHI, ELEPHANT BABY

Illustrated by

JOHN BUTLER

VIKING
PUFFIN

The sun rose slowly over the African plain, a glowing ball of fire hanging above the shimmering ground. Lorato lifted her great head, looking and listening for danger. She was the oldest elephant, the leader of the herd. That night her daughter Neo had given birth to her first calf. There was now a new member of the herd to protect.

Neo was standing a little apart from the other elephants, resting under the branches of an old baobab tree. Little Bashi leaned against his mother's legs. She stroked him gently with her trunk. He was full with milk now and wanted to sleep.

After a while, Lorato signalled to Neo that it was time to move on. Keeping the little calf close to her, Neo joined the rest of the herd. Bashi trotted beside her, still a little unsteady on his legs. Two of Neo's younger sisters took up positions behind the calf to help shepherd him along.

The herd moved slowly along the well-worn track which led to the watering hole. Bashi soon grew tired, but each time he stumbled, willing trunks helped the little calf to his feet.

Out in the long grass, three strong, lean bodies lay crouched and hidden. Three pairs of hungry eyes caught sight of the little elephant. Silent and unseen, the lionesses began to follow the herd.

As the elephants drew near the watering hole, two warthogs grunted angrily, but moved quickly out of their way. Bashi followed his mother down the muddy slope, his little legs slithering, trying to stay near her. The elephants headed eagerly into the water.

Neo urged Bashi to follow a little further, but his legs seemed to be sinking into the soft mud. He sank deeper and deeper. He struggled to free himself, squealing anxiously. He lost his balance then, and toppled over. Neo tried to lift the frightened calf with her trunk. Other elephants moved closer to help her, but little Bashi was stuck fast.

Suddenly, from the bank, a deep rumble from Lorato warned Neo of a new danger. She looked up. She saw the lionesses. The nearest of the three snarled and leaped to one side, as Lorato charged.

The lionesses slunk back into the grass, keeping their distance and pretending not to be interested, but Neo knew why they were there. They were waiting and watching for her little calf, waiting for a chance to seize him.

Desperately now she tried to free him. Bashi was squealing frantically. The more he struggled, the deeper he sank. Neo began to dig underneath him with her foot. Then suddenly Bashi was free and on his feet again. Neo comforted her frightened calf, helping him back up the bank.

All the elephants closed around him. Little Bashi was safe
inside a great forest of legs. No lion could reach him now.

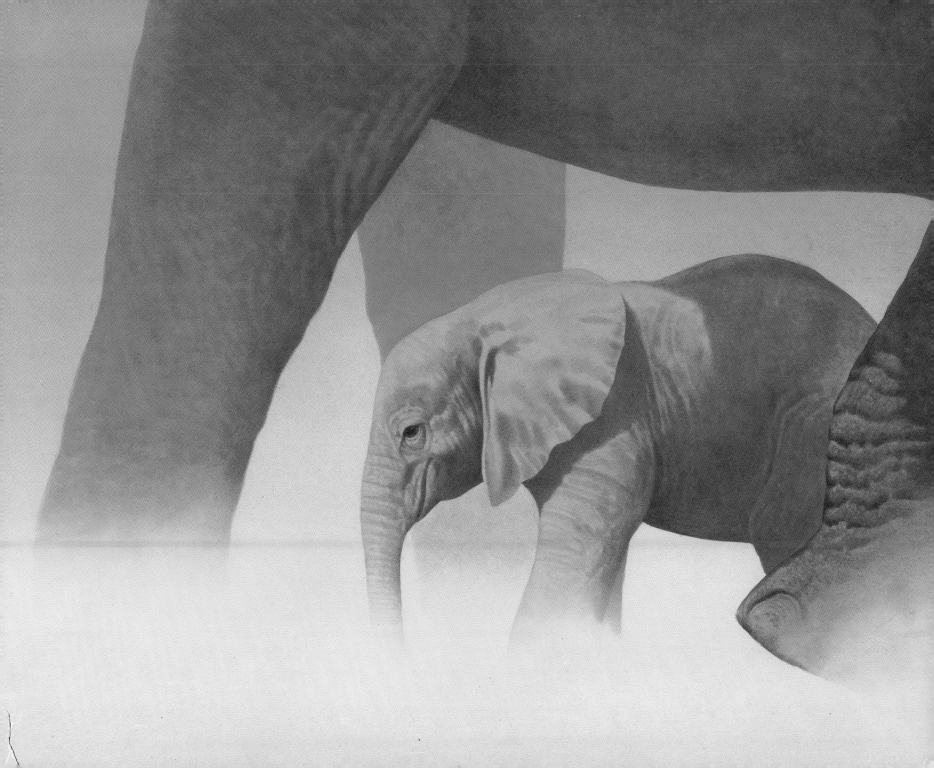

Lorato led the herd back to the great plain. Soon the little elephant could rest and sleep again. He would lie down in the long grass beside his mother. Bashi had survived his first day.